SRA

MW01690379

Thousand-Mile Words

By

Hilary Mac Austin

Illustrated by

Kate McKeon

McGraw Hill SRA

Columbus, OH

SRAonline.com

Mc Graw Hill SRA

Send all inquiries to this address:
SRA/McGraw-Hill
4400 Easton Commons
Columbus, OH 43219

Printed in the United States of America.

ISBN: 978-0-07-611293-7
MHID: 0-07-611293-4

1 2 3 4 5 6 7 8 9 MAL 13 12 11 10 09 08 07

The McGraw·Hill Companies

Contents

1 ◆ Talk to Me 1

2 ◆ Taku's Haikus 8

3 ◆ Haiku Moments. 16

4 ◆ Tied in Knots 21

5 ◆ Echoes 30

6 ◆ Stepping Word to Word . . . 38

— Chapter 1 —

Talk to Me

Tino sat in the very back row of the classroom. He stared hard at the floor. He wanted to be invisible. No such luck. The teacher, Mrs. Furman, looked at him.

"Class, Valentino Ishiro is a new student at our school. I want you all to welcome him," she said with a warm smile. "Valentino, can you tell us something about yourself?"

This was what Tino had feared. He hated being called on. He didn't want to talk in front of everyone.

Tino had always been quiet. He had always been a little bit shy too. But he hadn't always had so much trouble talking aloud. That started after his dad left.

Tino's dad had moved back to Japan last year. He didn't explain why. Tino didn't understand why he left. Tino's mom tried, but she couldn't explain it either. Tino didn't hear from his dad at all. He didn't write or call.

Tino and his mom had just moved to a new town. They moved because his mom was going to college. That was good for her. It was her dream. She had worked hard to get into college. And the whole family was proud of her.

"Tino," he mumbled to the class. He kept looking at the floor.

"Stand up, dear. Now, I didn't catch what you just said. Could you repeat it?" Mrs. Furman asked.

Mrs. Furman was old. She wore big glasses and had her hair in a bun. She had on an old-fashioned dress and really thick, heavy shoes.

Tino sighed and stood up. He was really tall for his age—almost six feet. Some of the kids in the class started to giggle. He heard a few whispers.

"It's Tino," he said a little bit louder. He didn't say anything else. The room got very quiet. All the kids were looking at him. Tino looked at the floor. He felt frozen. He couldn't get any other words out of his mouth.

"Can you tell us anything about yourself?" Mrs. Furman asked.

Tino just shook his head.

"Your mom told me your family is from Japan. Have you ever been there?" Mrs. Furman asked.

Tino shook his head again and didn't say anything.

"Well, where did you go to school before? Would you like to tell us about that?" she asked.

Tino shook his head again.

*"When will she stop?" he thought.

Finally she did.

"Well, thank you for letting us know that you like to be called Tino," Mrs. Furman said. "I want to welcome you to Woodhaven Middle School. I am your homeroom teacher, and I am also your English teacher. I look forward to seeing you in class. I am sure you'll do well here."

"Yeah," Tino mumbled as he sat back down.

Mrs. Furman gave Tino a sharp look, but she didn't say anything. For the rest of homeroom she left Tino alone.

Tino was called on in every class that first day. He knew most of the answers, and if the answers were only one word, he was okay. But if they were more than one word, he couldn't answer. He* just shrugged. Some teachers gave him sharp looks. Some sighed and shook their heads.

"Great," he thought. "Now they think I'm stupid. Well, that's okay. If they think I'm stupid, maybe they will leave me alone."

The problem was, *everyone* left Tino alone. Some kids stared at him in the halls between classes. Tino heard the word *weirdo* a few times, but nobody talked to him.

"Good," Tino thought. But it still made him feel alone. That first day was a long, long day. Tino couldn't wait for it to be over.

After school, Tino's mom was waiting for him at their new apartment.

"Hey, T. How did it go? Are the kids nice? Do you like your teachers?" she asked.

"Okay," Tino mumbled.

"Tino, talk to me. Please?"

"Just okay, you know, fine," Tino said. Tino knew his mom wanted him to talk more, but he just couldn't get the words out of his mouth. He couldn't figure out how to say what he was thinking.

His mom sighed.

"Well, that's good. I'm glad it went okay," she said, smiling. "Hey, guess what? There is a surprise on the computer. I think it will be better than okay. How about that?"

"Okay," Tino said, smiling at his mom. She tried so hard to make him happy.

— Chapter 2 —

Taku's Haikus

"Tino, look at this," his mom said. Tino peered over her shoulder. On the computer screen were the words:

Tino my cousin
Never met but want to know
I learn haiku—you? *Taku Ishiro*

"What?" Tino sputtered. He stared at the screen.

"This is from your cousin Taku in Japan. He's the same age as you. He lives in Kyoto. You can e-mail him every day and get to know him. He's learning English. You guys can be pen pals. Surprise!" Tino's mom said as she laughed and smiled at her son.

"What?" Tino sputtered again. "Why did he write like that?" He pointed at the screen.

"It looks like a poem. A strange poem, but still a poem," his mom replied. "Let's look up that word—*haiku.*"

Tino's mom looked up the word in one of her new college textbooks.

"Here it is. *Haiku* is a kind of Japanese poetry. It has only three lines. The first line has five syllables. The second line has seven syllables. And the third line has five syllables."

"Okay," Tino said.

"And there's more," his mom said.

Tino sighed and rolled his eyes. Now that his mom was in college, everything was a lesson.

"A long time ago, haikus had five lines. The syllable count was five-seven-five-seven-seven," she went on. "Then it changed, and people only wrote the first three lines."

*"Cool," Tino said. He was hoping that his mom was finally finished.

But his mom had more to say. Tino sighed again.

"Sometime later it went back to five lines. But this time there were two writers. The first writer would ask a question using the first three lines. The second writer would give an answer using the last two lines. Finally people stopped writing the last two lines. Now people just write three lines."

"Uh huh," Tino said. "Okay."

"So, are you going to answer Taku?" his mom asked.

Tino wasn't sure about this idea. Thoughts whirled in his head. What if his cousin knew his dad? What if his cousin liked his dad? What if his dad liked his cousin? What if his dad liked Taku better than* he liked Tino?

But his mom was so happy about this e-mail. Tino could tell.

So Tino wrote his first e-mail to his cousin.

Hey Taku. Haiku seems cool. Tino

He clicked *Send* and got up from the computer.

"No, no, wait!" his mom cried. "Let him e-mail back."

"Huh?" Tino asked.

"I worked it all out with your Uncle Hiroshi," his mom replied. "It's four o'clock in the afternoon here, so it's seven o'clock tomorrow morning in Kyoto. Taku can reply before he goes to school!"

"Wow," Tino thought. "That's cool." Just then a new message showed up on the computer screen. He clicked on it as fast as he could.

Can it be haiku

We will use to write our thoughts?

Birds flying through air

"What a weirdo," Tino thought, laughing to himself. "Just like me, I guess." Tino was beginning to like this idea—a cousin his age who was in Japan. And he didn't have to talk aloud to him!

So Tino began to type his first haiku. He counted the syllables on his fingers. He wasn't sure if he was doing it right, so he tried to make it simple.

Haiku I will try

But do not know how to do

So maybe not good

As Tino clicked *Send*, he felt nervous. What was he getting into? What if Taku didn't think his haiku was good enough? What if Taku didn't understand what he wrote? What if Taku wanted to talk about Tino's dad?

Tino almost didn't want to read his cousin's reply. But he did.

My new cousin friend
You do haiku good—fast too
Words simple and true

Tino felt a huge sense of relief. Taku had understood. And he thought Tino's haiku was okay. Before Tino could reply, Taku sent another e-mail.

I must start my day
As you end yours, think of me
Dreaming of freedom

Tino thought he and Taku seemed a lot alike. Tino imagined Taku sitting in a classroom. In Tino's mind, Taku was staring at a large clock. He was waiting for the long day to end.

Tino typed one last e-mail. It took him a long time. He tried different ways of putting words and sounds together. Many didn't work. Finally Tino had written a haiku he liked. He wrote "For Taku at the end of the day" on the subject line. Then he wrote:

Free when the bell rings
No questions, no answering
Stand, walk, run, fly, dream

— Chapter 3 —

Haiku Moments

*The next day at school Tino went to the library. He read books about haikus. He learned that haikus were about more than just syllables. They were about one moment in time. They made the reader think about the world. Tino read as many haikus as he could find. Some were silly. Some were beautiful. And some he couldn't understand at all.

Tino liked haikus. They were simple. They didn't waste words.

For the rest of the day Tino paid more attention to his teachers and his classmates. He was looking for "haiku moments." By the end of the day he had a few ideas.

A new message was waiting when Tino got home. Taku called it "My Day."

Sit, learn, and repeat
Sunlight shines through a window
The dust is dancing*

"He's good! I can picture him sitting in his classroom," Tino thought. "I guess I should write now." Tino tried to write something deep. But he couldn't get the words right. Then a picture of a girl he had seen at school came into his mind. Tino called his haiku "Girl at My School."

Brown hair and glasses
Old backpack, old jeans, old shoes
No one talks to her

Tino didn't know if this was a good haiku or not. He didn't know if Taku would like it. But he was really surprised that it was so easy to write.

Taku answered him right away. He called his next haiku "Boy at My School."

Loud, big teeth, big mouth
Feet that smell like rotten fish
Makes teacher crazy!

Tino leaned back in his chair and laughed. He tried to make his next haiku sound like Taku's. He called the haiku "Science Teacher at My School."

Mr. Solomon
Short, bald, bearded, big belly
His voice scratches glass

Taku replied:

Teacher Tanaka
Tall, thin, looking down at me
A crane eyeing fish

"How does Taku do that? That last line is great," Tino thought as he read the haiku. "I'm going to try writing about Mrs. Furman."

It took some time, but finally Tino had it.

Old Mrs. Furman

Small, wide, watching everything

An owl not moving

Tino didn't think his last line was as good as Taku's. "But at least I thought of the right animal!" he said to himself.

Tino and Taku spent the next half hour trading haikus about their teachers and classmates. For Tino, writing the haikus got easier and easier. And he couldn't believe how much he had noticed about the people in his school.

"This really feels like we're talking to each other," Tino thought.

— **Chapter 4** —

Tied in Knots

Tino and Taku had been e-mailing each other for a month. They wrote about the music they liked. They wrote about their favorite movies and video games. They wrote about their lives.

Tino had learned a lot about Taku's life. And Taku had learned about Tino's life too. Well, Taku had learned about *part* of Tino's life. Tino never mentioned his dad. Neither did Taku. Tino was relieved about that. Taku didn't know about Tino's trouble with talking, either. Tino kept that part of his life to himself.

E-mailing Taku was the best thing in Tino's life. But the rest of his life wasn't so good.

*Tino was quiet in all his classes. He listened, but he almost never answered questions. And he never asked any.

His teachers weren't happy about this. That was no surprise. They asked him why he wasn't joining in. But Tino couldn't talk about it, so he just shrugged. The teachers started to lose patience. They thought he was trouble. They started to complain about his attitude. At least that's what Mrs. Furman told him one day.

She stopped Tino in the hall.

"Tino, I need to see you after school. We need to talk about your attitude," she said.

"Yeah," Tino mumbled, looking at the floor.

"Stop mumbling!" Mrs. Furman said. "Remember, three o'clock sharp."

“What is her problem?” Tino thought. “I said, ‘Okay.’ ”

At the end of the day,* Tino walked into homeroom.

“Mr. Ishiro, we need to talk,” Mrs. Furman said.

“Uh oh, here we go,” Tino thought.

“Several of your teachers have complained to me about your attitude. They say you are rude. You mutter and mumble. You give one-word replies. You sit in the back of the classroom. And you never even look up. You do not show them respect.”

"Um . . . sorry," Tino mumbled.

"I don't need sorry," Mrs. Furman said, "I need to see a change."

"Yes, ma'am," Tino said with a sigh.

"And don't you sigh at me!" she told him.

Tino was worried. The school might call his mom. He couldn't let that happen. She had enough to think about. Why couldn't they just leave him alone?

"Big test comes too soon!"
Teachers nagging, "Work harder!"
Dark clouds gathering

The e-mail from Taku greeted Tino when he got home from school. Tino thought of Mrs. Furman and the other teachers. Teachers nagging? How true! Dark clouds? You bet!

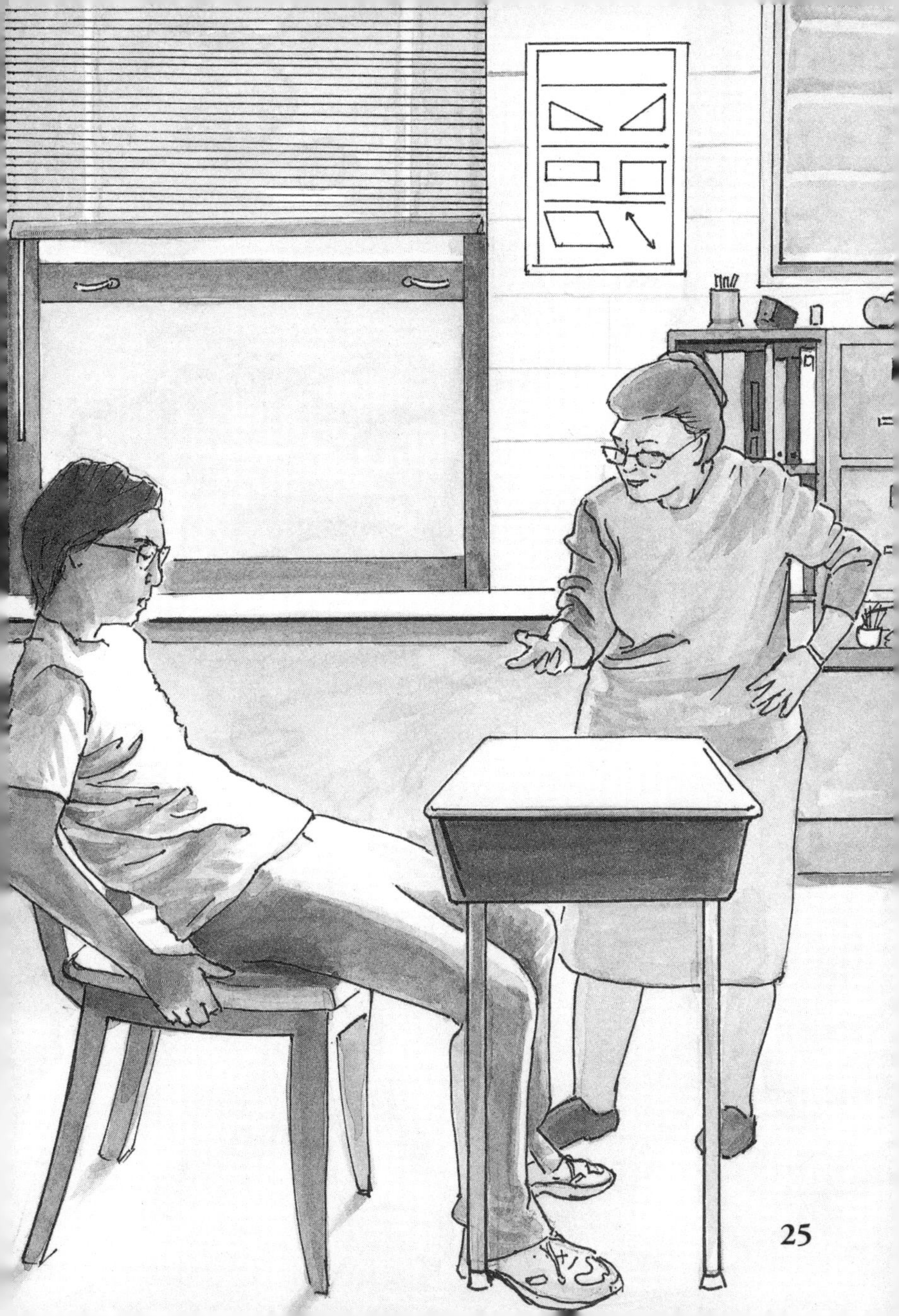

He replied to Taku's message.

Today the old owl

Flew straight at her silent prey

"Talk more!" she hooted

Then Tino remembered something. He had never told Taku about not talking. Tino sighed. He had better explain it now that he had written that haiku. It took some time, but he finally worked out what he wanted to say.

I'm silent all day

My thoughts are stuck, trapped inside

Knots I can't untie

Taku replied:

Stuck? All tied in knots?

But your thousand-mile words stretch

Across the ocean!

Tino stared at the screen. He was stunned. Taku was right! His words weren't tied in a knot when he wrote to Taku. When he wrote, he took his time and worked out his thoughts. But could he do that in school? Could he do that without haiku? Tino shook his head. No, it wasn't possible.

Then Tino thought of something. What if he kept the idea of haiku, but didn't worry about the syllables? It might be worth a try. He didn't want the school to call his mom. Tino wrote to Taku about his idea.

The next day in science class, Mr. Solomon asked for an example of a food chain. Tino thought of one. But could he say it aloud? Could he talk in front of everyone?

Tino made a deal with himself. All he had to do was raise his hand. Maybe Mr. Solomon wouldn't call on him. Then he wouldn't have to talk. He raised his hand a little. He didn't raise it very high. He was hoping Mr. Solomon would not see him. But he did.

"Yes, Tino?" Mr. Solomon asked.

Tino had never been more nervous. What if no one could hear him? What if he was asked to repeat himself? Even worse, what if everyone laughed at him? He shut his eyes and took a deep breath.

"Simple. Just a few words. Just say it!" he thought. "Get it over with."

Sun feeds the grass
Grass feeds the deer
Deer feeds the wolf

Tino whispered his answer. He looked down the whole time. He tapped the syllables with his fingers. It helped him concentrate.

Tino finished speaking. There was silence.

“Good!” Mr. Solomon said. Tino looked up in surprise. Some of the kids in the class were looking at him, but they weren’t laughing. Mr. Solomon asked another question and the class went on. No big deal.

“Whew,” Tino thought. “That wasn’t too bad. That wasn’t bad at all. I can do this. I think I can really do this.”

— Chapter 5 —

Echoes

*For the rest of the week Tino used his "haiku method." The more he used it, the easier it was to speak. He answered questions in more classes.

Sometimes he wrote important words in his notebook. That helped too. Then he would think about what he needed to say and turn it into a haiku-like poem. His plan was working.

Talking more in class also helped Tino with his classmates. Some kids still called him "weirdo," but now other kids nodded at him in the hall. Mrs. Furman even saw the change in Tino.

"I hear your attitude has improved this week. Good job," she said to Tino on Friday. Tino smiled.

That afternoon Tino e-mailed Taku as usual. Tino loved Friday afternoons. It was Saturday morning in Kyoto then.* He and Taku could e-mail for a long time because Taku didn't have to leave for school.

As Tino sat at the computer, he realized he was happy. He was talking to his friend Taku, and he had solved his problems at school.

Tino looked at his mom. She was studying. Books covered the table. A haiku came into in his head. He sent it to Taku.

Across the room, Mom
Leans over her book, frowning
Tugging words from it

Taku replied:

My dad watches me
Worries about my future
Makes me worry too

Tino read the first words of the haiku. Then he stopped. He got up and ran out of the apartment.

A few minutes later Tino's mom went outside. She saw Tino sitting on the curb. He was drawing in the dirt with a twig. She sat down next to him.

"Tino, I read Taku's last e-mail. Can we talk about it?"

Tino shook his head. He didn't want to talk about it—*ever.*

Tino's mom twisted a twig in her hands. "I'm mad at him too. But we've got to remember something. Your dad isn't a bad man. He . . . just couldn't stay. He missed Japan too much. He felt empty here, you know?"

"I think we have to talk about it," his mom said. "Your dad . . ." She sighed. Then she took a deep breath. "I know you miss him. I miss him too. And I know you're mad at him."

Tino shook his head again. He hadn't looked up once.

"No, you're right," she said, laughing softly. "I don't know either. Did you know we talked about moving to Japan?"

Tino finally looked at his mom. He shook his head again.

"We did. It was the year before he left. But it costs a lot to live in Japan. We didn't think we could make it work. So we decided to stay here. I guess he just couldn't do it."

They sat in silence for a while.

“You know,” Tino’s mom said, “I don’t know much about your dad’s family. But I do know that Taku didn’t mean to hurt your feelings.”

Tino nodded.

“Try to explain it to him. He’s been a good friend to you.”

Tino sighed and nodded again. They both got up and went back into the apartment. But Tino didn’t know how to explain it to his cousin.

Tino sat back down at the computer. There were three messages from Taku waiting for him.

The first was a haiku, just like always.

Are you still out there?

I wait for you—hear nothing

Wind whistles, echoes

The next one wasn't a haiku. It said:

Hey, are you okay? What is happening?

The last one said:

HELLO???

— Chapter 6 —

Stepping Word to Word

Tino sat down and stared at the screen. He didn't want to think about his dad. It was like reaching into a deep well—a well filled with dirty, muddy water. How could he explain that to Taku?

"I'll just start with why I left," Tino thought. He took a deep breath. His hands were shaking.

I see "dad"—I run

Away from a world with dads

Away from my thoughts

While Tino waited for Taku to reply, his mind raced. He felt so stupid. Taku wasn't even talking about Tino's dad. Taku was talking about his own dad. And Tino had run away like a little kid. Now Taku probably thought Tino was being mean. Tino just knew it.

Then a new e-mail appeared. It was more formal than any other e-mail Taku had written.

I bow to my friend

To forget this pain was wrong

True friends stand stronger

"Whoa," Tino thought. "Taku doesn't think I'm being mean. He thinks *he* did something wrong. No way." He typed his reply right away.

NOT YOUR FAULT TAKU!

I MUST STOP HIDING AND SPEAK

THE WORD I HATE . . . dad

Tino looked at what he wrote. All he wanted to do was make Taku feel better. He hadn't thought about what to say. The words had just poured out of him. But what he wrote was true. He did have to stop hiding. And he finally had someone to talk to about it—Taku, his friend. And Taku understood.

Tino knew he could finally ask Taku the question he had been so afraid to ask.

Do you know this man?

Once DAD, but now not—now what?

Who is he now—who?

Taku's reply came back right away.

I do not know him

Uncle—father's brother—is

A silent shadow

Taku didn't know Tino's dad? Tino couldn't believe it. Suddenly everything changed. They weren't laughing and sharing jokes without him. Tino's dad didn't like Taku better. Tino felt like a huge weight had been lifted off his chest.

Tino wrote Taku another e-mail.

There is a deep well
He left—it fills with anger
Why is he silent?

Taku replied:

My father tells me
Of a man silent in shame
In his own deep well

*Tino read the e-mail again and again. He had always imagined his father was happy in Japan. Tino imagined his father was relieved to be away from him and his mom. He imagined his father laughed and spent time with Taku and the rest of the family in Japan. But Tino's dad was not just silent with Tino and his mom. He didn't talk to *anyone*. He was hiding. He was ashamed.

"Mom," Tino called softly. "Look."

Tino's mom came over and read the e-mail.

"Your uncle never speaks of him," she whispered. "I thought he was being kind by not bringing up your dad. I'm so sorry."

"You're sorry? Why?" Tino asked in surprise.

"Because I should have talked to you. But I was hiding, too, I guess. I* didn't want to think about your dad."

"Me either," Tino said.

"I miss him," she said.

"Me too."

"You should write to him, you know."

"Nah," Tino said.

"No, you should. He is silent. But you aren't. Just look at your haikus. They are beautiful." She looked at Tino. "I think he would really like them."

Tino rolled his eyes at his mom.

"No, he would," she said. "And anyway, you need to tell him how you feel, T. Tell him what you're thinking." She pointed at the computer. "Now you have a way."

"Well, maybe . . . ," Tino said. "Maybe I'll try."

Tino turned back to the computer. His mom smiled.

"I know you will, T. I know you will," she said. She gave him a kiss on the head and returned to her books.

Tino wrote Taku a new e-mail.

I will try to cross

The space between him and me

Stepping word to word

Taku replied with only two lines. He completed Tino's thought with his own. It was like the old haikus.

And reaching into a well

With all your thousand-mile words

Tino smiled and began typing his first haiku to his father.